NICKY'S LOPSIDED, LUMPY BUT DELICIOUS ORANGE

PHYLLIS GREEN

NICKY'S
LOPSIDED, LUMPY
BUT DELICIOUS
ORANGE

Addison-Wesley ▲▼

Text Copyright © 1978 by Phyllis Green
All Rights Reserved
Addison-Wesley Publishing Company, Inc.
Reading, Massachusetts 01867
Printed in the United States of America
ABCDEFGHIJK-HA-798

Book designed by Charles Mikolaycak

Library of Congress Cataloging in Publication Data

Green, Phyllis.
Nicky's lopsided, lumpy, but delicious orange.

SUMMARY: Thinking that her inadequacies have caused
both her father and stepfather to live away from the
family motivates Nicky to strive for perfection in all
she does.
[1. Family life — Fiction] I. Title.
PZ7.G82615Ni   [Fic]   78-4599
ISBN 0-201-02590-6

for my son, Bruce

NICKY'S LOPSIDED, LUMPY
BUT DELICIOUS ORANGE

* I *

Nicky Politan stepped on the San Rafael, California, school bus at the corner where Ridge Drive meets Eliza Way. Nicky looked pretty much like she had the day before because she still wore the purple dress with white trim. Her brown hair was still growing out of the wedge cut and her blue Adidas were still beat-up looking. There was one difference. She held her wrist at a special angle to show off something new buckled on it. A Donald Duck watch.

Alex Politan, her new father, had made a passing-through visit during the night and left it for her as a surprise.

"Why didn't you wake me up?" she had asked her mother.

"He left this for you," her mother said.

Nicky opened the box. It had not been wrapped. Inside, she found the Donald Duck watch.

9

She laughed as she fastened it around her tanned wrist.

"It's wacky," she said.

"Alex will be disappointed. He thought at least you'd say it was quacky," her mother said.

Nicky threw back her head with a giggle. "Oh, that's awful!" Then suddenly she was serious again. "Mother, why didn't you wake me?"

She sat beside Gay Clover in the third seat behind the driver. Nicky thought she was going to die if Gay didn't notice the watch. She made a fuss of studying Donald Duck's hands.

"I sure hope we get to school on time," she said. "I'd sure hate to be late."

"Are we late?" Gay asked, her popping eyes peering through her long bangs.

"According to my new Donald Duck wristwatch, Mrs. Miesenmeyer better drive like crazy."

"Yeah, right over the hill. Did you say your watch was new?"

Nicky shook her head "yes" and held the watch in front of Gay's bangs.

"It's cute," Gay said.

Nicky's insides felt like warm sticky glue.

"Thanks," she proudly grinned.

The first person at Sun View School to notice was, of course, Ernestine Ring, who noticed everything.

"Hey, let me wear it at recess," she begged Nicky.

"Well. . ." Nicky said, wanting to be nice but wanting to wear the watch herself.

"I'll be careful," Ernestine insisted. "What could happen to a watch?"

Nicky wrinkled the freckles on her nose. But she said, "O.K."

She watched Ernestine carelessly fasten the watch on her dirty wrist then run off to the monkeybars.

Why couldn't I have said no? Nicky thought. *Why does she always get her way with me?*

"Ernestine, I've changed my mind," she called. But Ernestine ignored her, running off to the swings.

She lost sight of her then because Gay came up to talk. But suddenly Ernestine was there with her stringy hair saying, "Look what happened to this cheap watch!"

"What happened?" Nicky asked, a sick feeling enveloping her.

"The minute hand fell off," Ernestine said, with a giggle in her throat.

Nicky grabbed the watch. "Oh, Ernestine, did you do this?"

"I didn't do anything. It's a dumb watch."

"It is not!" Tears were at the edges of Nicky's green eyes.

The bell rang. Recess was over.

Nicky frowned and found it hard to concentrate in school. *I'll never, never let Ernestine have anything of mine again,* she thought. But she knew it to be a weak thought. Ernestine had gotten her way with Nicky for the six years they had been in school together. Ernestine always had a sad story. She made Nicky feel sorry for her. Then she begged and begged, and Nicky would end up giving in to her.

When they were first and second graders, Ernestine had told Nicky she was too poor to bring milk money. So every day Nicky picked up her carton of milk then passed it on to Ernestine to drink when they got outside to the picnic tables where everyone ate lunch. Nicky's mother, who had been Mrs. Forrest then, had a fit when she found out. She told the teachers, and after that, they always watched to make sure Nicky drank her milk and didn't give it away.

After school, Ernestine caught hold of Nicky's elbow while she stood in line for the school bus to take her back up the hill.

"It's my brother's birthday," Ernestine said.

Nicky wished she could rudely say "So?" but she smiled at Ernestine and said, "How old is he?"

"I forget. But he's not getting any presents. Not one. My mother can't afford to buy him one. Isn't that awful?" Ernestine said in her scratchy voice.

"That's too bad," Nicky said.

"Your watch is broken," Ernestine said.

"I *know*," Nicky said.

"Well, if you lend it to me, I'll get it fixed. Then I'll give it to my brother for a birthday present. Then he'll be happy. Then I'll bring it back to you tomorrow, and he'll think he lost it. And it won't be any worse for the wear."

"I don't know," Nicky said. She did like the idea of getting the watch fixed before her mother saw it broken.

"C'mon," Ernestine said. "Gimme it."

"It's so complicated."

"C'mon," Ernestine repeated, taking the watch off Nicky's wrist.

"What will I tell my mother?" Nicky called to the running Ernestine.

"There's your bus!" Ernestine yelled back.

The yellow bus pulled into Cherry Lane and stopped in front of the line of waiting children. *Darn you, Ernestine Ring,* Nicky thought. *You better get that watch fixed and fixed right.*

Nicky's mother, Lisa Politan, was in the kitchen working on a canvas. She was an artist. A real artist. Sometimes she sold an oil painting. Sometimes she talked before ladies' groups about art and famous artists. Lisa Politan even looked like an artist, or maybe more like an artist's model because she was beautiful. She was just a little bit taller than Nicky, who was five feet tall, and she had long dark hair and big brown eyes and curvy lips. She was so pretty she didn't even have to smile to be pretty. She always wore bright colors or things like the leopard print slacks and red blouse she had on when Nicky got home from school.

"Whatcha painting?" Nicky asked.

"What's it look like?" her mother teased.

The picture was a landscape of the California seashore at Carmel. Lisa liked to paint in the kitchen, paint and cook at the same time. It all got so intertwined, Nicky was sure her mother would end up putting American Vermilion or Alizarin Crimson in the tuna fish salad in place of mayonnaise.

"Well," Lisa said, "I trust old Donald Duck made a big hit at school today?"

"Oh my gosh!" Nicky said, grabbing her wrist.

"What?"

"Oh darn! I left it in my desk. Oh what a dope I am. Gosh. How could I be so stupid? Well, I'll get it tomorrow."

"I hope you didn't lose it. Alex got it especially for you."

"I can picture it right now beside my math book." Nicky closed her eyes and nodded her head up and down. "Yes, there it is, right beside my crummy, old, red math book."

"Well, good. Don't forget it tomorrow," Lisa said.

Nicky opened the patio sliding door, picked a yellow lemon off the bush there, rubbed it on her purple dress, and then chomped into it.

"How can you *do* that?" Lisa asked.

"Why didn't you wake me up last night when Alex was here?" Nicky asked her mother as she chewed.

Lisa worked on the landscape. "It was late," she said.

"He really comes around a lot," Nicky said dryly.

"Try to understand," Lisa said softly.

"He comes around at night like a sneak thief."

Lisa dropped the paint brush. "Darn," she said. She picked it up and pointed it at Nicky. "That's a rotten thing to say. Alex is your father."

"I can't help it if he adopted me. I can't help it if my real father deserted you. I can't help it if you married a priest. I can't help any of it. I just wish. . ."

"He was around more often?" Lisa asked.

Nicky sat down at the kitchen table. "I guess so. He's never around. What kind of father is that? Why couldn't we have had a normal family? I like things to be normal. I don't like to be deserted and divorced and remarried to a priest."

"Hey," Lisa said, "those are the things that happened to *me*, not *you*."

"I know. It just seems like they happened to me. I mean, they sort of have, haven't they? I mean, I've been *here*. I've felt all that. I feel so . . . oh, I don't know. Forget it! When's he coming back? Is he ever going to claim us?"

"Hey, do you like the colors in this tree?" Lisa asked.

Nicky got up and walked around to see the canvas. She looked at the bending tree that had been pushed and pushed by the wind off the sea, the way all the trees look at Carmel.

"Why don't you put a little more of this there and that here and this other over here," she said, pointing to the various shades of green on Lisa's palette.

"Darling, I think you're right. I caught the wrong angle of light. Bless you, you'll be an artist yet."

"Did I say something right? I was just kidding! Honestly, I think it looks absolutely perfect the way it is."

"My paintings are never perfect, remember that. And I do think your suggestions are good ones. And I don't know when he'll be back, but I know, I just know, some day he'll claim us."

"Hey, Mom, are you crying?" Nicky asked.

"Oh, Nicky, I love him so much."

"Oh, Mom, I'm sorry."

Lisa blubbered and waved her green fingers at Nicky. "I'd hug you if this darn oil paint was washable."

That made them both laugh because they both knew just how much Lisa hated to do the wash. There were always piles and piles of it collecting in the garage.

* 3 *

That night it was hard for Nicky to get to sleep. She kept thinking about her Donald Duck watch and Ernestine and *had Ernestine gotten it fixed by now?*

"Can I get a drink of water?" she called to her mother, who was painting in the kitchen.

"You mean you aren't asleep yet," Lisa said. "Well, O.K."

Nicky got the water in the bathroom and then she went back to bed.

What a lumpy pillow, she thought. Then she rubbed her foot.

"My foot's asleep but I'm not," she said.

Then she wondered if Alex would come that night.

"Mother, do you think Alex will be here tonight?" she called.

"Nicky! Honestly! Go to sleep."

She rolled over on her stomach. Her arms hit the bedpost. Lisa came running to her bedroom.

"What happened? What was that crash?"

"Oh, I just knocked the bedpost. By accident," Nicky said.

Lisa turned on the blue lamp on the vanity. She sat on the edge of Nicky's bed.

"What's up, kid?"

"I can't get to sleep."

Lisa felt Nicky's forehead.

"Sore throat?"

"No."

"You seem cool enough."

"I'm just tossy-turny."

"Well, just tonight. Don't think it's going to become a habit. Put your robe on and come watch me paint," Lisa said.

"Really?" Nicky said, sitting up.

"Just tonight. Remember."

Nicky flew out of bed. She threw on her pink robe and practically skipped to the kitchen.

"Can I have something to eat? I'm starving."

"You really know how to take advantage of a situation, don't you?" her mother said. And to Nicky, that meant that she could have something. So she made a bowl of corn flakes.

"Stop slurping," Lisa said. "You sound like two pigs."

"I really like that Carmel scene. I hope you don't sell it so we can keep it. Wouldn't it look neat above the table here? Look," Nicky said, unhooking the picture of the white rabbit, "let's put the white rabbit in the bathroom and the Carmel scene here."

"Hey," Lisa said. "Uh, put the rabbit back, Nicky."

"Gee, look at the hole in the wall," Nicky said. "I've heard of bank vaults behind pictures but, wow . . . That's an ugly hole."

"That's why I covered it up, Miss Brain," Lisa said.

Nicky hung the white rabbit picture back on its hook.

"How did the hole get there?" she asked.

"It got there. Somehow. I forget," her mother said.

"You look funny," Nicky said.

"Maybe because you should be asleep, and I should have peace and quiet to get this painting done," her mother said, her face getting pinker and pinker.

"I don't care if you don't want to talk about it. I'm sorry I lifted the white rabbit. I'm sorry I saw the stupid hole."

"Nicky, I think I can sell this painting for three hundred dollars if someone will shut up and let me paint it."

"O.K.," Nicky said.

It got very quiet in the kitchen. Lisa stared at her painting, but she didn't seem able to touch the brush to it.

"Did you throw something at Alex?" Nicky whispered.

Now Lisa's face was red.

"*I* didn't do it!" she said, exasperated.

"You don't have to tell me," Nicky said. "I guess Alex threw something at you."

"Oh, for heaven's sake," Lisa said. "Oh Nicky."

"He did, didn't he?"

"No, *he* didn't."

"Oh. Well. Why can't you tell me then? I don't understand why you can't tell me."

Lisa turned to the refrigerator. "I'm sorry, Mrs. Fraser," she said to it. "Your painting would have been finished but my daughter couldn't sleep one night and asked me a lot of stupid questions."

Nicky laughed. She looked at the refrigerator. "Really, Mrs. Fraser, I take all the blame. There's this ugly hole in the wall, see. And mother doesn't want to talk about it. Why do you suppose it's there, Mrs. Fraser?"

"Mrs. Fraser thinks it's an old ugly hole. She thinks perhaps it's five years old. She thinks it's hard for your mother to talk about it because it was put there by someone she loved at the time. On the night he went away," Lisa said, almost unable to get the words out.

"Oh," Nicky gulped. "My father. My real father."

Lisa nodded.

"How?" Nicky whispered.

"He rammed his fist through the wall," Lisa said.

"Was he trying to hit you?"

"No. He had perfect aim. He was trying to hit the wall."

"Wow."

"I think he broke his wrist. It was wobbly. But I don't know for sure because I never saw him again."

"I was in first grade," Nicky said. "I remember him."

"Oh, yes. Rennie was memorable," Lisa said. "He was the type of guy I always fell for. A handsome, sexy bad boy. Even in high school, I always flipped for the bad boys. My mother would say, 'Lisa, they'll hurt you. They'll use you and hurt you. Why don't you go out with a nice boy for a change?' If she could only have lived long enough to meet Alex she would have known I got my nice boy at last."

"Why was my father bad? Because he left?"

"He wasn't all bad. I loved him, remember, and you did too. But he never really acted married. He did what he pleased. If he wanted to drink too much, he did. If another girl interested him, he'd go out with her. If he wanted to buy anything, he bought it. He didn't like responsibilities. Family. Bills. Oh, he hated bill time. This house was his prison. So he broke through the wall one night. And went away."

"He couldn't fit through that hole," Nicky said.

"Just his fist went through the wall. It was symbolic. He took off in his red pick-up truck with his motorcycle tied to the back. I went out to the street and watched him go. He got smaller and smaller; then the truck went around the curve, and that was it."

"Didn't you try to stop him?"

"I think so. I'm not sure. I didn't know he was going away for good. I thought. . ."

"I'd have stopped him," Nicky said.

"Would you? Well, I survived. And now I have my nice boy. It won't be long, Nicky, honest. Alex will tell them he's married, and he'll get a regular job, and we'll be just like a normal family. You'll see."

Nicky smiled. "That will be nice," she said, but she thought, *how desperate must you be to punch a hole in the wall?*

"Mrs. Fraser," Lisa said, "you'll have to wait. I can't paint another stroke tonight. I'm going to bed. C'mon, kid," she said to Nicky.

"What did he say when you asked if Alex could adopt me?"

"It was all done through lawyers."

Lisa turned out the light. She put her arm around Nicky's shoulders as they walked down the hall.

"Look, little buddy," she said, "your father was a dreamboat. You have to understand, he wasn't made for family life. He was like a caged animal. He just had to break free. It was his *nature*. Now we have found another love who will take care of us. It's been a bouncy life, but we'll make it. Right?"

"Right," Nicky said. She hugged her mother.

"Good night, Mom."

"Good night, doll," her mother said.

* 4 *

Nicky and Gay sat together on the school bus. Gay's big eyes strained to see through the bangs.

"What time does Donald Duck say today?" she asked Nicky.

"Gay, are you on dope?" Nicky said.

"Why?"

"Where were you yesterday when Ernestine practically ripped it off my arm so she could give it to her brother for a birthday present?" Nicky said.

"I don't know," Gay said.

"You were standing in the bus line *right in front of me.*"

"I didn't see anything," Gay said.

"You never see anything! As long as I've known you, you've never seen anything! I don't know how you do your schoolwork. Why don't you *ever* get a haircut?"

Ernestine wasn't on the playground before school. She came in late, when Mrs. Ketcher was halfway through the math lesson. Nicky tried to get her attention by pointing to her wrist and looking mean, but Ernestine ignored her.

Nicky could hardly wait for recess. She cornered Ernestine.

"O.K., Ernestine. Where's my watch? You promised."

"Hey, my brother really liked it. I couldn't get it fixed, but he liked it anyhow. It was the best birthday party ever. We had balloons and streamers and chocolate cupcakes and little blue favors filled with party nuts."

"Well, where's my watch?" Nicky said, exasperated.

"I don't know. He hid it. I said, 'Look, fink, I just borrowed the watch so you could have a nice birthday and now I have to give it back.' He just kicked me in the shins and now he's hidden it."

"Well, you've got to get it!" Nicky said.

"My brother said, 'Finders, keepers, losers, weepers,'" Ernestine said, a strange sort of smile beginning at the end of her upper lip.

That did it. Nicky bopped her on the head with her fist. Ernestine was momentarily stunned, but her thick head wasn't hurt. She recovered and whacked Nicky in the ribs and tripped her at the same time.

Nicky went WOMP! to the ground, landing squarely on her rear end.

Gay rushed over, trying to peer out of her bangs. "What's wrong, Nicky?" Gay asked.

"Get back," Nicky ordered. "Ring is a dirty, double-crossing, watch-stealing thief. She's going to get what's coming to her."

Nicky stood up, and then the real fight began. Punches were thrown, ankles were kicked, feet were stomped on, and hair was pulled out. Once when Nicky kicked her foot out at Ernestine, the foot struck Gay, who was bending over trying to stop the fight.

"Ah — you — ouch — ooo," Gay screamed, clutching her forehead. Blood dripped out from under the bangs.

Nicky ran to Gay, and Ernestine ran away.

"Oh Gay. Oh Gay. I'm sorry," Nicky said. "I meant that for Ernestine. Let me look."

She tried to part Gay's bangs, but Gay said, "Go away. I'm O.K. Leave me alone."

"But there's *blood!*" Nicky said. She pulled Gay's bangs apart and held them above her forehead.

"Oh my gosh, Gay," Nicky whispered and quickly let the bangs fall back into place.

"It's just a little cut," Gay said.

"You mean I didn't do all that?" Nicky asked.

"It's a birthmark," Gay said. "I didn't ever want anyone to know. Will you tell?"

"Gosh, I won't. How did it happen?" Nicky said.

"I don't know. When I was born, I think. It's

27

getting a little smaller, I think, but it just about covers my forehead. Don't you hate the color?"

"Well, I don't know. I never saw one before. But I like colorful things. It's sort of purple and red and blue. Maybe you shouldn't keep it covered. Maybe you should show it every once in a while so everyone can get used to it. It's kind of distinctive, like a beauty mark," Nicky said.

"Well I don't *want* to show it. You won't tell will you?"

"O.K."

"Promise?"

"Promise."

* 5 *

The first thing Nicky did when she got home from
school was say to her mother, "Did you know Gay
Clover has an enormous Alizarin Crimson birthmark all over her forehead?"

"Yes," Lisa said.

"Well nobody at school knows, and she made
me promise not to tell."

"Nicky!" Lisa said.

"Well, I'm sure she just means *kids*. I'm sure I
can tell my own mother."

"I guess you remembered your watch today?"
Lisa said.

"Well, there's a problem," Nicky began. She
told her mother that Ernestine had tricked her
again.

"Honestly, Nicky, *Alex* gave you that watch.
Are you going to be led around by people all your
life? That Ring girl has conned you for years. You
must be No. 1 on her list. Anytime she wants

29

something she knows old Nicky will come through."

"Well, I don't like people to be mad at me. I like to be liked."

"She doesn't *like* you when you give her things. She must regard you with contempt. Honestly, the whole thing just makes me sick."

"It makes me sick, too. Honest. I loved that watch."

"Oh, honey," Lisa said. "Then why do you always let her get her way? You're just too nice. It's possible, you know, to be too nice. Well, listen, are you going to have a painting lesson today?"

"O.K. I want to work on that still life I started last time."

Nicky set up her easel and got out her beginner's set of oil paints. She also found her 12 × 18 canvas board and placed it on the easel.

"Ready," she said.

"You're not wearing a smock today, Miss Mess?" her mother asked.

"Oops, I forgot." She ran to get her yellow smock.

"O.K.," Lisa said. "Now, you see before you oranges, lemons and grapes in a bowl and a red-and-white-checked tablecloth. Now, before you put a smidgeon of paint on that canvas, I want you to look at this Marc Chagall reproduction. We all need inspiration. Would-be artists must study master artists like would-be musicians study Bach and Bacharach, like would-be writers study Shakespeare and Oates. We're going to study Chagall, Matisse, Dufy, Schoonover, Wyeth — all of them. We don't want to copy them. That would be pointless, like cheating at Solitaire. We want to learn from their genius and grow from there. O.K.?"

"O.K."

"Now, this painting by Chagall is titled *To My Wife*. Now study it and tell me what you see."

Nicky looked at the Chagall. "I see a naked lady with hair on her thing," she said.

"Color!" Lisa said. "I want you to look at his colors! They are brilliant, varied, vibrant. Chagall is the master of *color*. I want you to do for color on your still life what Chagall has done for color in *To My Wife*."

"You mean I have to paint hair on my orange?" Nicky said.

"Nicky," Lisa said.

"I was only teasing. I really like the whole painting. It's wild!" Nicky said.

"All right. Study it. Then paint color into that bowl of fruit like you've never painted before. Mix. Experiment. Be daring. Be colorful. You'll have dull areas and bright areas. And if you do it right, your still life will come alive. Then, in other lessons, we'll go on. You'll probably paint that bowl of fruit in fifty different ways. Now you'll paint color. The next time, shapes and shadows. You'll paint it as it looks, and you'll paint it as it feels, and then as it smells. You'll paint the bowl of fruit sitting upside down on the ceiling, then you'll paint it falling about the room, then hiding in the corners. You'll paint it so much you won't want to eat fruit for a year. But when you're done, you'll *know* that fruit. You'll have mastered it. You will have control for putting it on canvas in any way you want. You'll be a little bit more of an artist than you are today."

"But, will I be fruity?" Nicky asked.

"Begin," Lisa said. "I'll peep over your shoulder every so often."

Nicky painted for about an hour before Lisa came back to check.

"The color isn't bad," said Lisa, which, coming from her, was almost a compliment. "But what have you done to that poor orange? You made it ROUND, perfectly *round*. Have you ever looked at an orange? Have you ever seen a perfectly *round* orange? That looks like a nursery school version of the sun. I have never seen a more perfectly round orange. You couldn't have made a more perfect circle if you had used a compass."

"I sure could have used one. I thought I'd never get it right," Nicky said.

"Well, it's awful," Lisa said. "Look at this orange. Hold it. It isn't perfectly perfect. It's a . . . funny shape."

"Gee, it is. I thought oranges were round."

"You thought! You've got to look!" Lisa said.

"I like things to be nice and neat and perfect. I like my really round orange. I think it's perfect."

"The only thing it is is perfectly awful," Lisa said.

"But you like the color," Nicky said.

"It's not bad," Lisa said.

"I'm going to give this painting to Alex when it's finished," Nicky said.

"Why, Nicky," Lisa said. "That's nice. He'll like that."

"Even with a perfect orange in it?" Nicky teased.

Lisa laughed. "Even with that. He loves you."

"When's he going to tell the bishop he's married? When's he going to take us down to the San Joaquin Valley to live with him?" Nicky said.

"Baby, he *wants* to tell the bishop he's married. But he knows the church won't accept it. He'll have to leave. He *would* leave now for us. But he hates to let down his parishioners. They've known him all his life. They believe in him. They believe priests shouldn't marry. It would be shocking to them. He's going to tell them. He will tell them. Someday. We have to be patient. He has to figure out a way to tell them so they won't be hurt. So they won't be disappointed in him. He doesn't want his work among the migrant workers there to fail either. If he leaves the parish now, all the things he's worked for with them might go down the drain." Lisa sighed.

33

Nicky was quiet for awhile. Then she started to put her paints away for the day.

"You know," she said to her mother, "Alex is sort of like Gay. He covers us up like she covers up her birthmark."

* 6 *

The next day at recess, Nicky and Gay ran to the seesaw.

"Let's see if we can get balanced," Nicky said.

It wasn't so easy because Nicky weighed more than Gay, but finally she moved up and Gay moved to the end of the seat, and they were balanced.

"My dad comes home tonight. He's been in Boston," Gay said.

"Nice," Nicky said.

"Will your new dad be home tonight?" Gay asked.

"I don't know," Nicky said.

"Why don't you ever know? My dad always tells my mother where he is and when he's coming home."

"Well, Alex sort of surprises us because he can't always get away."

"From where? Where does he work?" Gay asked.

"I can't say," Nicky said.

"What is he, a spy or something?" Gay asked.

"Oh no, he's a . . . Can you keep a secret?"

"You *know* I can! I've never told that you peed in your first-grade desk. I never told that you loved Arthur Max in second grade. I never told Mrs. Finley you threw up in the third-grade wastebasket. I never told . . ."

"O.K. O.K. But this is the most *secret* secret I've ever told you. It's practically a matter of life and death. Do you solemnly promise never to reveal it, that is, until the certain party reveals it himself, which, at that time, you may feel free to say you already knew because you are my best friend?"

"Good grief. I won't tell your secret if that's what you mean. I just won't tell. I promise," Gay said.

"Lean close," Nicky whispered.

Gay moved close, and Nicky's side of the seesaw thumped to the ground.

"Ouch!" Nicky yelled.

Gay shrugged her shoulders. "I'm sorry! I forgot we were on the seesaw."

"Let's go over by the eucalyptus tree," Nicky said, getting off the seesaw and holding it for Gay.

When they got to the tree, Gay said, "Well?"

Nicky pulled a strip of bark off the eucalyptus.

"Alex, my new father, is a Catholic priest."

Gay stared out at Nicky through her bangs.

"Do you know anything about priests?" Nicky asked.

"I know they don't get married," Gay said.

"That's right. But Alex did. It's a secret. I mean, everyone knows my mother is Mrs. Alex Politan, but you see, he's a priest far away in southern California. We just didn't tell anyone up here he was Father Politan. And he adopted me and everything. Of course, the lawyers know and the judge knows, but he hasn't told his church yet."

"When will he?" Gay said.

"Well, he will. But I'm not sure when. Because then, you see, when he tells, he won't be a priest anymore. He'll be an *ex-priest*."

"Did your mother meet him at confession?" Gay asked.

"They met at a wine and cheese party. Priests are people. They just don't spend their whole lives sitting in confession boxes. My mother had a little too much wine and started telling Alex all her problems. Then she brought him home to see her paintings and before they knew what was happening . . . Zamm! Love."

"Boy, is he going to get in trouble," Gay said.

"Yeah. It's a whopper. He not only married a woman. He adopted a daughter."

"I'd hate to be in his shoes."

"Oh, Alex is brave," Nicky said.

"Maybe God will strike you down for being part of it all."

"Hey, what are you trying to do? Scare me out of my wits? Maybe God will strike you down because you're in on the secret."

Gay clutched her throat. "I'm already in enough trouble with Him."

"Why?"

"Because I've said, 'God damn you, Grandfather, you are a knucklehead.'"

"Really? Out loud?"

Gay nodded. "Don't you dare tell my grandmother. She'd be madder than God."

The bell to end recess rang. The girls walked toward their classroom door.

"Is he handsome?" Gay asked. "Are you afraid of him?"

"Well he doesn't come to visit us looking like a priest. He wears regular clothes. He's not handsome handsome. He's nice looking. Sometimes he smokes a pipe. He has sideburns. He looks like a real person."

"I'd feel funny about it," Gay said.

"Alex wouldn't let you. He'd like you right away, and he'd make you giggle and feel silly, and you'd want to just laugh all day you'd feel so good."

"He sounds nice," Gay said.

"Shh . . ." Nicky said, as they got near their class line. She whispered, "Sometimes my mother kisses and hugs him. She's just crazy about him. They're a cute couple."

"My mother is taller than my father," Gay said.

"Oh, not my mom and Alex. They're perfect," Nicky said.

* 7 *

Back in the classroom, Mrs. Ketcher announced they would be having an art contest.

"The basis for the contest is American history," Mrs. Ketcher said, straightening her blue print blouse and attacking one of its buttons that had opened. "Think back over the course of American affairs and depict some scene which you feel to be extremely significant. There will be prizes for the best posters. The judgment will be equally divided between artistic and historical significance."

Nicky shuffled her feet under her desk. She was excited. She loved art and she loved history. Ideas were racing through her head. She just had to choose one. It would be difficult.

"I'm going to give you some time now," Mrs. Ketcher said. "Perhaps fifteen or twenty minutes to get inspired. Look through your history book. What means something to you? You can choose from the very early history of our country to the most recent issues of the day. Poster boards are at the back of the room. Pick one up and take it home with you today. *Don't bend them.* Bus children can roll them up so they won't get mangled on the bus. I should say neatness will count, too, in the judging. Well, I guess if I stop talking you can get on with your inspiration."

The noise of desks opening and books being taken out filled the room.

"Feel free to use the encyclopedias," Mrs. Ketcher said. "Oh, did I say the prizes will be small cash awards?"

"Oh-h-h - h!" the class sighed.

"So do your best. And now I really will let you become inspired," Mrs. Ketcher said, smiling and again buttoning that slippery button on her blouse.

Nicky didn't know where to begin. She wanted to do about *twenty* posters. She thought of a fantastic scene about the witch trials in old New England. She thought of doing the Battle of the Alamo, the Gold Rush in California, a scene from the Depression. She thought of doing the astronauts stepping off onto the moon, but she figured a lot of boys would do that. What she really wanted to do was something that no one else in the classroom would think of. Something small, but significant.

She paged through her history book and got lots of good ideas but not *the* idea. So she went to the encyclopedia corner and started looking through them. She thought awhile about the signers of the Declaration of Independence, Paul Revere's ride, and then she thought about doing a poster on Betty Friedan as sort of a women's lib thing.

Harold Pitman finished with the M encyclopedia and asked if she wanted it.

"I'm looking for the T," he said.

Nicky traded him the T for the M. She found her idea in the M book *just* before Mrs. Ketcher said, "Time's up."

Nicky would do her poster on General Douglas MacArthur, the day he was fired by President Harry Truman.

Mrs. Ketcher had a strict rule about not taking encyclopedias home, so Nicky worked on her poster at school during recesses. There was a small picture of General MacArthur in the encyclopedia but it was only of his head. Nicky planned to draw him from head to toe, how she felt he looked that day in April, 1951, when he was told to come home from Korea. He had disagreed with the president and had spoken out when he was told to be silent. He had been a famous general of World War II. He was popular with the people. But he disobeyed, and he was brought down by the president. Nicky wanted to show him disappointed and defeated and desperate. She had him standing tall as a soldier stands. She had him looking tough, but disappointed. She had him making a fist with his right hand as if he could . . . punch through a wall with it.

She wanted the American flag to be somewhere in her poster. But everywhere she tried it, it didn't look right. And then she tried the red, white and blue as reflecting in General MacArthur's eyes. One white star fell out of his left eye as if it were a tear.

Her poster went faster now. It was right. She knew it. It was good. She knew that, too. She finished in four days of recesses, and she could hardly wait till the posters were hung and judged.

Nicky didn't think she could stand the day of judging. She was a nervous wreck on the school bus. Gay had done what she, herself, termed a stupid rendition of Benjamin Franklin's kite being struck by lightning.

"I'll get last prize," Gay said.

"Your kite was pretty nice," Nicky said.

"Yes, but when I was all done my father informed me Benjamin Franklin probably didn't have a kite with Superman's picture on it. Oh, you'll win, Nicky. Everyone knows that. Yours is fantastic," Gay said.

"I'm awfully nervous," Nicky said.

When they got to school they saw there was, indeed, a ribbon on Nicky's poster.

"Second prize," Nicky read, whispering. Her heart felt like it had jumped up and clogged her throat.

"Who could have won first?" Gay demanded. "Nobody's was as good as yours."

42

They discovered first prize was won by Harold Pitman's collage of the first Thanksgiving.

"He must have cut up two hundred of his mother's November magazines," Gay said.

"There's glue everywhere," Nicky said.

"Would you look at *that*," Gay said. "He's stuck a cooked turkey on *top of a Pilgrim's hat!*"

Harold Pitman won five dollars. Nicky won three dollars, and John Parsons won one dollar for his poster of an astronaut taking the first step on the moon.

Nicky had a hard time all day to keep from crying. She kept telling herself, "Mine's the best. I know it's best because I'm an artist. Mrs. Ketcher is just a person, so she can't possibly know what is artistic and what isn't. Harold Pitman is a nice boy, but he has made a messy, unartistic collage."

If only Mrs. Ketcher had not asked her to stay after school, she probably wouldn't have cried at all. But Mrs. Ketcher did ask her, and when Mrs. Ketcher asked her if she had *traced* the picture of General MacArthur, Nicky did cry.

The other children were gone.

"I only ask if you traced it because it is so nearly perfect."

"I'm an artist. I don't need to trace. The picture was from the encyclopedia. You can see for yourself it was real small. I made it big."

"But it's so almost perfect," Mrs. Ketcher said.

"It *is* perfect," Nicky said.

"Well I can't change the prizes now. You got second. That's quite good. Don't you think Harold's collage is good?"

Nicky wanted to scream, "It's LOUSY," but she wiped her eyes and said, "Well, I sort of think it's interesting that he pasted the cooked turkey at the top of a Pilgrim's hat."

"Yes," Mrs. Ketcher said, "that struck me, too. Right away."

Nicky found Gay waiting for her outside.

"We better run," she said.

"Don't bother," Gay said. "The bus left without us."

"Hey, thanks for waiting for me," Nicky said.

"I figured you needed me. C'mon, I know a shortcut home," Gay said.

* 8 *

"We'll go in back of these houses, then up the hill. There's a path," Gay said.

"How do you know this way?" Nicky asked.

"Sometimes I come down to the store for my mother, if she forgets bread or something. Ernestine lives here," Gay said, pointing at a redwood fence they were passing.

"Really?" Nicky asked. She stopped and looked through a hole in the fence. "Hey, there she is. The whole family, I guess, is in the back-yard."

Gay found a place to look through the fence too.

"The Ring's only have four kids, but the way they run around and get into trouble it seems more like forty."

"Do you see any of the boys wearing my Donald Duck watch?" Nicky asked.

"They probably sold it already," Gay said.

"Oh Gay, look at Mrs. Ring. *What* does she have on?"

"I can't see."

"Well part your bangs. It looks to me like a white bra and yellow underpants."

"In the backyard?" Gay asked.

"They're drinking beer," Nicky said.

"They look like people that don't brush their teeth. *She* looks like a lady wrestler," Gay said.

"She's chubby but not that chubby," Nicky said.

"Maybe it's the underwear that makes her look fat. Wouldn't she look great riding on the elephant in the circus wearing a purple bra and pants?"

"And the elephant wouldn't mind *too* much," Nicky said, giggling.

"Shh . . ." Gay said.

"Did you dig another hole in this yard?" Mrs. Ring shouted. "I almost broke my ankle in it." She was talking to Ernestine's four-year-old brother. He looked whiney and grubby, and his nose was running.

"No," he said.

"Yes you did!" Mrs. Ring said. "I've seen him," she told her husband. "He digs these deep holes. He's looking for a mole. Next thing you know I'll break my leg in one."

"I didn't do it," the little boy said. "The mole did it."

"You put the dirt back in that hole right now!" Mrs. Ring said, loud enough for the whole neighborhood to hear.

"I won't."

Mr. Ring got up from the picnic table and whacked the kid on his bottom.

"Yes you will. Dammit," he said.

"Let's go," Gay said. "They're fighting. It's messy. It's awful."

They walked away from the fence.

"Yes, but they're a real live family. I'd give anything to have a family that started together and stayed together," Nicky said.

"But you have a real family now. You're adopted by the priest and everything. Can't you be satisfied with that? Here's the path."

"I guess I will be satisfied when we're all together for real," Nicky said.

"If you want to see a perfect family, just look at mine," Gay said.

"But your father's always away."

"Well he's an executive. He flies all over the country."

"But he's never home," Nicky said.

"Well, I think we're perfect, and I guess that's all that matters."

They were beginning to puff, going up the steep hill.

"This is some shortcut," Nicky said. "I may not make it."

"I'm used to it," Gay said.

"Then why are you out of breath?"

They stopped to laugh and rest.

"O.K., onward," Nicky said. "Listen, stop at my house on the way home, and I'll show you something."

Gay stood inside the kitchen, and Nicky lifted the picture of the white rabbit from the wall above the table. The ugly hole stared out at them.

"My father, my real father, did this," Nicky said, solemnly.

"Did he do it with his head?" Gay asked.

"He probably would have liked to, but he used his fist. It broke."

"Boy, these houses are really securely built," Gay said, sarcastically.

"I guess they were too secure for my father."

She put the white rabbit back on its hook.

Lisa came into the kitchen. She was wearing a pink blouse and white shorts.

"Hi girls! I was next door at Glad's. Well, how was school? How was the art contest? Want some cookies?"

Gay went to the sink. "I just need a glass of water, then I'm going home."

"C'mon, how was the art contest?" Lisa asked, gaily.

Nicky poked her hand into her blue slacks pocket and brought out three dollars. She held them up for her mother to see.

"Second prize," she said, smiling.

"Goodbye," Gay said, walking quickly to the front door.

"You're kidding," Lisa said. "Second? After what you told me about your poster? It sounded beautiful. Who was first?"

"You don't know him. Harold Pitman."

"I know little Harold."

"He did an interesting collage about the first Thanksgiving."

"You sound like the perfect good sport," Lisa said, sarcastically. "Remember the saying 'the best man always wins'? Well, it's not true. The best person doesn't always win. But the best person keeps trying."

"I know," Nicky said, biting her lip.

"What say we go out to dinner, sport?" Lisa said, making a fist and tucking it under Nicky's chin.

Nicky hugged her mother. "O.K., Mrs. Sport," she said.

That night before she went to bed, Nicky tried to kick in the wall. But she hurt her big toe. She held onto her ankle and hopped on one foot, trying not to cry out. When it felt better, she got an idea.

She found Old Teddy Bear at the bottom of her clothes closet. He was faded brown. He had one beady little black button eye and a seam in his stomach was ripped open so his white stuffing was seeping out.

Nicky took him and whacked him against the wall. Then she swung him hard and wrapped him around the bedpost. Then she beat him against the mattress. Then suddenly, she fell on the bed and hugged Old Teddy Bear.

She pulled the green cover up and lay back on the pillow and bathed Old Teddy Bear's face with tears.

"Oh Teddy, Teddy, Teddy. That stupid Harold Pitman won first prize."

When she finally fell asleep, Old Teddy Bear was soaked and still in her arms.

* 9 *

A couple of days later, at last recess, Gay told
Nicky she wouldn't be on the school bus going
home.

"Are you going to clean the board erasers
for Mrs. Ketcher?" Nicky asked. "If you are, I'll
stay and help."

"I'm going to smoke a cigarette with Bony
Alison and Ernestine Ring."

"You're not!" Nicky said.

"I just said I was," Gay said.

"Gay, this isn't like you."

"But I've always wanted to smoke."

Nicky kicked at the pebbles on the playground. She caught a few on the top of one of
her beat-up Adidas. She stared at Gay.

"But you hate Ernestine," she said.

Gay caught hold of the flagpole and whirled
around it. Her plaid blouse billowed out behind
her like a parachute.

"I know. But she has the cigarettes."

They walked over to the swings. They both jumped on a swing and started pumping.

"Gay don't go," Nicky said.

"Look, your mother smokes," Gay said.

"But I'm trying to get her to stop. It gives you cancer, Gay."

They were both swinging very high now but they weren't together, and some of their words to each other sounded loud, and others were so soft they could hardly hear them.

"Sometimes you're too good TO BE TRUE," Gay said. "WELL, COME ON with us and just WATCH."

Nicky decided to pump harder to see if she could go up over the top. It was a school rule that you weren't allowed to, but everyone tried it. As she pumped higher and higher, she realized there was nothing she could do to stop Gay. *One person can't control another person. You have to let them go. Like my real father. There was nothing my mother could do. She had to let him go.*

When it was time to go back in school, Nicky told Gay that she would go along . . . just to watch.

They met after school under the eucalyptus tree. Nicky. Gay. Ernestine. And Bony Alison. Bony Alison was a thin girl who got the name Bony because every part of her looked like elbows. Her wrists looked like elbows. Her shoulders and knees looked like elbows. Even her chin looked like an elbow.

"This will be my third smoke," Bony Alison said, proudly.

"Where are we going to do it?" Gay said.

"What's she doing here?" Ernestine said, pointing at Nicky.

"I'm just watching," Nicky said.

Ernestine looked relieved.

"And taking notes for the surgeon general," Nicky added.

"How many cigarettes do you have?" Bony Alison asked.

Ernestine held up three fingers.

Now Nicky was relieved. Ernestine couldn't talk her into trying a cigarette if she only had three. And she looked so greedy about them Nicky was pretty sure she wouldn't even want to share a puff.

"Who's got the matches?" Ernestine demanded.

"I do," both Gay and Bony Alison said.

"It's lucky the school didn't burn down," Nicky muttered.

"We can't do it here," Gay said. "Where do we do it?"

Ernestine led them two blocks away to a small fenced-in section behind the beauty shop. They sat crowded amongst five garbage cans.

"Everything smells like permanents and hamburgers," Nicky said. "There are flies."

"How do we do it?" Gay asked. "I've never tried."

Nicky poked Gay. "Better watch out that your bangs don't catch on fire."

Ernestine and Bony Alison had already lit up.

Bony Alison puffed away like a madwoman. "Oh, is this great! Wow." *Puff.* "I love this brand." *Puff.*

Gay almost burned her fingers with the match. "This darn thing won't light. I can't get it started."

"Suck in when the flame hits the end," Ernestine said, blowing a smoke ring.

Bony Alison looked admiringly at Ernestine's smoke rings. "I wish I could do that," she said. But when she tried smoke rings, they just came out funny looking.

Nicky laughed because she thought Bony's smoke rings looked like wobbly elbows.

Gay's cheeks were all sucked in, but nothing was happening.

"Tell me what to do," she begged Ernestine. "I've tried and tried. There must be something wrong with this crummy cigarette."

"Here, hold mine," Ernestine said. Then she lit Gay's cigarette and handed it back to her.

"Oh, thanks. Now what?" Gay asked.

"Now suck it in and puff it out."

Gay sucked in the smoke. She sucked and sucked like she was eating a strawberry soda. Nicky could see her eyes popping out between her bangs and getting bigger and bigger and looking panicky. Suddenly she exhaled.

A big cloud of smoke covered her face. Gay threw down the cigarette, and Bony Alison immediately grabbed it up. Gay got up and staggered to a garbage can, lifted the lid, and was sick into it.

"I'm dizzy," Gay said. "I'm sick."

"You went too fast. Take a little at a time," Bony said, handing back Gay's cigarette.

"Oh no," Gay said. "That was enough for today. You can have it," she graciously told Bony.

"Gee, thanks," Bony Alison said. She put the cigarette out and dropped it into her jeans pocket for future use.

"You can smoke it when we're done with these," Ernestine said. "I have one more cigarette I was going to smoke later by myself. Now we can smoke our second cigarette together."

"O.K.," Bony Alison agreed. "I love to smoke. Let's try to do this at least once a week," she said to Ernestine. "Do you think you could get two cigarettes a week?"

"Oh sure," Ernestine bragged. "We can be almost chain smokers."

Nicky looked at Alison. "Smoking once a

week is a dumb thing to do, Alison. You'll have elbows all your life. That you can't change. But now you'll have yellow teeth and bad breath."

"I don't feel so hot," Gay said. "I think I'll go home and lie down."

"I'm going too," Nicky said.

Ernestine and Bony Alison didn't even stop puffing to say goodbye.

As they picked their way between the garbage cans and got out the fence gate, Gay whispered, "Why did you let me do it?"

"You made me," Nicky said.

"But how could I do something with Ernestine? I hate Ernestine," Gay said.

"Let's just say you went berserk for the moment. There are some people who can talk anyone into anything, and Ernestine is one of those people."

* IO *

The next week the sixth grade at Sun View School had a field trip planned to the San Francisco Zoo.

"Do you have your dollar?" Lisa asked Nicky that morning.

"Yes."

"Do you have your permission slip and your lunch?"

"Roger."

"O.K. Have a good time. I may be down at the school later on in the morning. I'm Hot Dog Day mother this month, and I have some details to work out with my committee. But I suppose you'll be gone by then," Lisa said.

"I think the bus leaves at 9:30," Nicky said.

"I won't see you till after school then. Have fun. Don't stick your head out the bus window or in a lion's mouth."

Gay and Nicky were lined up waiting to go into their classroom when Ernestine came up to them. She was crying.

Gay and Nicky looked at each other. Gay moved her head back and forth in an emphatic NO gesture.

"I lost my permission slip," Ernestine bawled.

Gay and Nicky didn't say anything.

"I've never been to the zoo!" Ernestine blubbered. "This is the first time I've had a chance to go. In second grade I got chicken pox the day before our field trip to the zoo. And now I've lost my permission slip."

"Why don't you run home and get another one?" Nicky said.

"I wanted to, but Mrs. Ketcher won't let me. She says I don't have time. My mother will kill me."

"Why?" Gay said.

"Because she *expects* me to be at the zoo, and I won't be there. She'll kill Mrs. Ketcher too. She'll kill the principal too. She thinks this school is pretty dumb to begin with. Now she'll really be mad."

"Well, you're the one that lost the permission slip," Nicky said. "Why should she take it out on Mrs. Ketcher and the principal and the school?"

"If you'd ever seen my mother when she's

mad, you'd know." Ernestine started to cry so hard her shoulders were shaking.

Nicky looked at Gay. Gay shrugged her shoulders.

"She'll beat me too. She kicks so hard. And she'll make me sleep in the garage. And she'll only feed me soup for dinner. Cream of spinach soup."

"Oh for heaven's sake, Ernestine. What do you expect us to do about it?" Nicky said.

Ernestine wiped her eyes. She looked at Nicky. "Are *you* going to the zoo?"

"Yes! Everyone in the whole class is going," Nicky said, exasperated.

"I'll have to go to the library and read all day," Ernestine said.

"Well, that's not so bad. There are lots of good books."

"Would you like to go to the library and read all day?" Ernestine said.

"I wouldn't mind."

"Then let's change your permission slip to look like it's mine!" Ernestine said.

"I didn't mean I *wanted* to go to the library," Nicky said.

"But you've been to the zoo and I never have. If you do it for me, I'll be your best friend," Ernestine said.

"*I'm* her best friend," Gay said.

"I'll be your second-best," Ernestine said.

"I'd really like you if you'd do this for me. Here, let me see your permission slip."

"I don't know," Nicky said.

"Don't do it," Gay said.

Ernestine took the paper and started erasing Nicky's name and her mother's name. She wrote instead Ernestine and Mrs. Ring.

"There, see how easy it was? Oh, there is something else . . ."

"What?" Nicky said just as the beginning school buzzer sounded.

"You won't need your dollar now. I left mine at home on my dresser. I'll pay you back tomorrow," Ernestine said, grabbing Nicky's dollar as they filed into the classroom.

"You dumb bunny," Gay whispered.

"Harold will collect your permission slips," Mrs. Ketcher announced as she took her white slip straps and hid them back under her blue dress. "Does everyone have a permission slip?"

"I found mine, Mrs. Ketcher." Ernestine was waving a permission slip over her head.

Nicky raised her hand.

"Yes?" Mrs. Ketcher said, fluffing her white hair.

"I don't have one," Nicky said.

"Why ever not?" Mrs. Ketcher said, adjusting her girdle.

"I have a little earache. It's so windy at the zoo. Mother thought I'd better not go."

"Well . . . I'm sorry. I'm afraid you'll have to

go to the library. I'll give you some assignments and then you can spend the rest of the time reading. I'm awfully sorry, Nicky."

"Oh that's O.K. I like to read, and I've been to the zoo."

Nicky got her assignments and left for the library. She was glad to get out of the classroom. She was afraid she would start crying in front of everyone. *Why oh why oh why,* she thought, *do I let Ernestine talk me into these things?*

Halfway through her math assignment she heard the school bus leave with her classmates on the field trip. She heard the shouting and cheers and happiness, and her throat got very tight. She closed her eyes and stuck her head into her math book.

At least I still have my lunch, Nicky thought. *Ernestine must have forgotten.*

That thought made her so happy, she stopped feeling sorry for herself and took the apple out of her lunch bag and ate it.

At ten o'clock the first-grade teacher poked her head in the door and asked if she'd like to help a few first graders with their reading workbooks. Boy, would she ever!

She loved being in the first-grade classroom and having the kids treat her like she was a very big person and quite important. But at eleven o'clock her job was done, and she walked back outside to go to the library again.

She had her hand on the library door when

she looked in the window and saw a group of ladies at one of the tables. The lady doing all the talking was Lisa Politan!

Oh my gosh, Nicky thought, *the Hot Dog Day mothers!*

She crouched down by the wall outside the library. *What am I going to do?*

* II *

Nicky started walking on her haunches away from the library door. She wanted to keep her head below window level. She came to a corner and went around it.

She heard a door open. *Oh, let it be the kindergarten door, not the principal's office,* she thought. Slowly, she looked up.

It was the principal, Mr. Foley, coming out of his office. He looked up at the sky as if to say "another beautiful day," then he breathed deeply, adjusted his horn-rimmed glasses, and turned toward her.

Nicky hugged her knees, looked down at the ground and tried to be invisible.

"Lose something, my dear?" Mr. Foley asked.

Nicky looked up.

Mr. Foley smiled at her.

"Hi, Mr. Foley," she said.

"Hi there, Nicky. What are you doing?"

Nicky stood up. She didn't know what to say.

"My class is at the zoo."

"And you're bored in the library," Mr. Foley said. "How would you like to be my secretary's helper? Mrs. Piney is bogged down today. She'll be glad to have some help. Tell her I sent you."

"Oh, Mr. Foley, thanks!" Nicky said as she ran to the principal's office.

Mr. Foley laughed and went on his way, which just happened to be to the meeting of the Hog Dog Day mothers where he just happened to mention to Mrs. Politan that Nicky was being his secretary which just happened to make Lisa burst open the principal's office door five minutes later to shout . . .

"WHATAREYOUDOINGHERE? WHYAREN'TYOUATTHEZOO?" . . . which just happened to make Nicky cry.

And eventually Lisa and Mr. Foley and Mrs. Piney got the whole story out of her about Ernestine and the permission slip and the dollar and the cream of spinach soup.

"Franklin, I have had it up to here with that Ernestine Ring," Lisa said, gesturing about two feet above the top of her head.

"This could be serious," Mr. Foley said. "If Ernestine gets in some sort of accident today, the school could be sued. Those permission slips aren't something we dreamed up. They're necessary for insurance purposes. In fact, I'm going to

64

drive down to that zoo and bring Ernestine back to school."

"See what you've done?" Lisa said to Nicky.

"I'm sorry! I'm sorry!" Nicky sobbed. "I didn't want to do anything wrong, but Ernestine makes me."

"There comes a time when you have to take a stand. You have to say a very small word. There are only two letters in it, and it is pronounced, *NO*."

Lisa fiddled in her purse until she found a cigarette. She lit it and started puffing furiously.

"And if you can't say *NO*," she continued, "then say *BUG OFF*. I'm sick of that Ernestine running your life, but I'm more sick of your letting her."

Lisa started pacing back and forth in the principal's office.

"I want to go *home*," Nicky sobbed.

Lisa looked at Mr. Foley. He nodded yes. So they packed up her books and put her in her mother's Volkswagen, and Lisa drove her home. Nicky went to bed and stayed there for two days. She just didn't want to get up. She didn't want to talk. She didn't want to go to school. She didn't want to see Ernestine. She didn't want to make another mistake.

She finally got up and talked and went to school and saw Ernestine. But she didn't make another mistake. She was very serious and worked very hard on school papers, and if she

65

didn't make 100% on all of them, she never got lower than 93%. And that 93% made her very upset, and she told herself it would never happen again. Nicky Politan was going to be absolutely perfect, and 93% was just not good enough.

* 12 *

Nicky continued her oil painting of the bowl of fruit. She never painted the fruit as it really was. The oranges were perfect round circles. The grapes were perfect round smaller circles, and the lemons were perfect ovals.

Lisa tried to encourage her to mar their perfection to make them a little more real.

But Nicky was stubborn.

"Every painter has a style," she told her mother, "and painting perfectly is my style."

Lisa snorted.

"There's a difference between having a style and being amateurish, and you're not the only painter who doesn't know the difference between the two.

"What's this big thing you have about being perfect? It seems to have ballooned since the zoo affair. Look, I don't want you to be perfect. Just be a person with virtues and faults. God knows I have my share of flaws. You can't be everything to everybody.

"You know, I have to laugh. Not so long ago you said Alex was like Gay because he covered us up. Well, do you know what I think? I think Alex is like you.

"He's afraid of not being a perfect priest. He fell in love. Priests are supposed to be above that. He turned out to be human, instead of perfect. And it's killing him.

"On the one hand he loves us. He wants to shout out to the world, 'Hey, look at this great girl I married! Hey, look at her wonderful daughter I adopted! Hey, look world, I'm a happy man!'

"But the other half of him is disappointed that he turned out less than perfect."

Nicky listened to her mother but she didn't comment. She just went on painting her perfect picture.

* 13 *

Alex surprised them one Friday night and announced he could spend the whole weekend with them.

Lisa hugged him, and he hugged Lisa. Then Nicky hugged him, and he hugged Nicky. Then all three of them hugged each other.

"We'll go to Novato tonight," Alex said. "They're having a carnival. We can eat there. Hot dogs. Things. We'll ride on the ferris wheel and those things that turn you upside down."

"Oh, that's great!" Nicky said. "I've always wanted to go on them, and Mom never let me."

"Oh, Alex, I don't know. . ." Lisa said. "It looks so dangerous."

He put his arm around Lisa. "What if I promise we'll go on them before we eat the hot dogs?"

"C'mon, Mom," Nicky said.

"Well, O.K.," Lisa said. "Oh, you two! Go ahead. But *I'm* not going on them!"

They got into the Volkswagen. Alex drove, and Lisa sat beside him, as close as she could get, and Nicky rode in the back seat.

Nicky thought, *Alex is really good for my mom. God probably figured He better loan him to her. She needed somebody so badly. Boy, we both needed him.*

"I've been talking to some of my friends who are ex-priests now," Alex said. "Some of them are teaching in Los Angeles. One of them sells real estate, and one sells insurance. I'm trying to figure out what I want to do. They're talking to their bosses about me. Maybe it won't be too long before I have a real job. A money-making job."

He looked at Lisa and smiled.

Nicky knew he felt bad about not paying for them, yet. But her mother made out for them with her paintings and mostly with the inheritance she had gotten when Nicky's grandmother had died. Lisa also taught art in night school at the college.

Lisa once told Nicky that Alex didn't know the value of money because he never had to handle it as a priest.

"I think I'm going to be telling them real soon. This is ridiculous," Alex said. "I want to be with you. I can't stand it without you. I'm the loneliest man in southern California."

Lisa cuddled closer to him. "Just be sure you get a job that you really want to do. I don't want you to rush into something and then be sorry."

He winked at her. "How could I be sorry if you're with me?"

"I mean it," Lisa said. "I know what you really love — your life's work, helping the migrants."

"Sure, I'd love to continue it as an ex-priest. But we could starve to death. I need a bankroll to support my projects."

"I can see the lights of the carnival!" Nicky said.

"There it is," Alex said. He turned off Route 101. "Let's see if we can find it by following the lights."

Soon they had parked the car. Alex took each of his girls by the hand and walked them into the carnival.

Nicky thought it smelled wonderful. All popcorny. She saw three girls with pink cotton candy and knew she'd have to have some of that before the evening was over.

They passed by a man guessing weights. The prizes were magic wands. *Hmm, I'd like to try that,* she thought. They came to the place where you test your strength by striking a hammer against a metal object, hoping you send the ball up to ring the bell.

"Oh, Alex, try it!" she coaxed.

"Not me. I'm a weakling," he said.

"Oh, c'mon, Alex," Lisa teased.

He took hold of the hammer and pretended he couldn't lift it over his head.

Lisa and Nicky giggled.

Then he swung it back and really walloped it down. The ball went up fast . . . up . . . up . . . and not quite to the bell, it sank down again.

They all laughed.

"Well, after my hot dog, I'll have more strength," he said.

"Oh, let's try this," Lisa said.

It was a booth where you placed a quarter on the month of the year. The man at the booth spun a wheel and when it stopped, the month where the pin landed won. The prize was a fat rubbery snake about as big as a boa constrictor.

"They look awful!" Nicky said, excitedly, putting a quarter down on January.

Lisa put a quarter on July. And Alex put one on May.

The wheel said August.

"Let's do it again," Lisa said. So this time they picked April, June and October.

"I have great faith in October," Alex said.

The carnival man spun the wheel.

"June," he called out in a bored way.

"That's me. June. That's me. I won!" Nicky said. "Look, I have June!"

The carnival man threw the big snake at her.

"Ugh. Oh gosh. Feel it. It's slimy," she said.

"It's wonderful," Lisa said. "See? Here, I'll drape it around your neck and waist. Good grief, it is long! Once more around your waist. What do you think Alex?"

"Nicole, are you sure he didn't say October?" Alex said, tickling Nicky.

Nicky thought she couldn't be happier. *Oh what a great night,* she kept saying to herself. *This must be the greatest night since I've been born.*

"Hey, a dime a dish," Alex said, coming up to the next booth. "Now there, Lisa. Feast your eyes on the beautiful china direct from the discount store. Now tell me what is your heart's desire. The little rose vase? That little fluted job? How about the glass saucer and cup?"

Lisa pointed. "The green candy dish," she said.

Alex adjusted his elbow and aimed carefully and sent a dime flying high. It landed on the dirt floor of the booth.

But he wouldn't give up.

"I'll get the hang of it yet," he said. "My true love desires the green candy dish. . ."

"The ugly green candy dish," Lisa said.

". . . the ugly green candy dish," Alex said, "and she will get it."

He tried fourteen times, and finally his dime went in the green candy dish and stayed there.

The carnival woman handed him the dish after first scooping out the dime.

"There," he said, blowing the dust off it and presenting it to Lisa with a bow. "Your twenty-nine cent candy dish. It only cost me a dollar forty."

"Oh look at those big stuffed toys!" Nicky said, eyeing the next booth. "See, you have to throw rings around those pegs."

"I'm good at that," Lisa said. "I even win at horseshoes."

"I didn't know I'd married an athlete," Alex said. "Now, how do we win one of those big stuffed toys?" he asked the carnival man.

The carnival man recited the rules in an unenthusiastic monotone.

"You ring three out of five you win a little plastic monkey. Ten monkeys you trade in for one of these here little stuffed toys. Ten little stuffed toys you turn in for a middle-sized stuffed toy. These here on the third row. Ten middle-sized stuffed toys you turn in for one of the big stuffed ones. Ten cents a try."

Alex looked at Lisa. "I wonder if it wouldn't be easier to just buy one for a hundred dollars?"

"You forget. I'm good at this," she said confidently.

Lisa began throwing rings. When she had spent three dollars and eighty cents, she only had two plastic monkeys to show for it.

"I give up," she said, laughing. "Here, Nicky, you always wanted two plastic monkeys didn't you? You can hang them from the mirror on your vanity dresser."

Lisa watched Nicky and Alex ride the ferris wheel and the Trabant. Then she closed her eyes and refused to watch when they rode the Dynamite Twister.

They ate hot dogs and french fries and corn on the cob and Pepsi and candy apples and pink cotton candy and popcorn till they wished they hadn't.

"What good is a carnival if you don't get sick?" Alex said.

They stayed till midnight.

"Midnight is beautiful," Nicky said. "Look at all the stars."

"I don't know how you can see them," Lisa said. "You're so tired your eyes are practically closed."

"Honest, I'm not tired," Nicky said.

But she fell asleep on the way home. Alex carried her into the house. Lisa helped her put on her pajamas.

"Oh, Mom," she sighed, "don't we have a wonderful family? Didn't we have a great time?"

She had one thought before she again fell into sleep. *My perfectness is paying off.*

* 14 *

They slept late Saturday morning, and when they woke, Alex informed them that he would cook breakfast.

"My specialty is fried eggs over easy. I drive our housekeeper wild. But then she doesn't know how to fry eggs. Do I have any takers?"

Both Lisa and Nicky said they would try them, and when they did, they thought they were delicious.

"But you put ketchup on yours," Alex said to Nicky.

"Think nothing of it. She puts ketchup on everything," Lisa said.

After breakfast they made a picnic lunch and drove out to Bolinas.

They sat on the beach and watched the tide come in and seep into the sand. Nicky collected a pile of slippery rocks and a few seashells to take home with her. She found a sand dollar that was almost perfectly round.

They walked up and down the beach, relaxed, happy.

When they came back to the blanket, a gray and white seagull had broken into one of the sandwich bags.

"Get away," Lisa said. "Shoo!"

The bird glared at them.

Alex swished the air in front of the seagull with his hands.

"Shoo! Shoo! Your mother's a Presbyterian," he said.

The bird jumped up and flew off.

They ate what was left of the picnic lunch. Then they took off their shoes and socks and waded in the water.

Saturday night Lisa and Alex went to La Petite Auberge for dinner. Nicky went next door to watch TV with their neighbor, Gladys.

On Sunday morning when Lisa and Nicky got up they found Alex, already dressed, sitting in the patio reading two Sunday newspapers.

Lisa yawned. "Did the newspaper boy deliver *two*? I thought you would sleep in."

"Couldn't," Alex said.

"But we got in so late last night."

"I've already been for a walk," Alex said. "I walked around up here on the hill. When I checked back, you still weren't up so I walked down the hill to the little grocery. I walked in and bought a paper. When I came home, I saw the same paper had been delivered. See how little I know about you?"

Nicky thought Alex looked funny. Like he was nervous. He kept looking at his watch. He read a little bit then got up and paced around the yard, then looked at his watch and sat down and read a little bit more.

Lisa was in the kitchen making pancakes.

"What's the matter with Alex?" Nicky asked her.

Lisa flipped a pancake. "Nothing. Why? Put the syrup on the table, baby."

"Is his ride coming this morning? He keeps looking at his watch as if he's late for something," Nicky said.

"He doesn't have a ride," Lisa said. "He's going to start to hitch about five o'clock this afternoon. He figures he'll get to the Valley by tomorrow morning."

After breakfast, Nicky still felt as if Alex was about to explode. She was lying on the beige davenport reading the Sunday funnies.

"Shoes off the davenport," Lisa said.

Nicky meant to kick them off, but what she was reading was so interesting she forgot.

"Shoes, Nicky," Lisa reminded.

And then Alex did explode. "Will you do what your mother says *when she says it?*" he demanded.

Nicky was so surprised, she dropped the paper and stared at him.

"Go to your room for fifteen minutes," he said.

Nicky slowly got up and walked to her room. She felt hot. And strange. How dare he come into their house and boss her around? And her mother *let him.* Who did he think he was, anyhow?

When she got to her room, she remembered who he was. He was Alex Politan. She was Nicky Politan. He was her father! The idea finally sank in. He was her father, and if he wanted to have fun like at the carnival, he could; if he wanted to yell at her, he could. *And he sure did yell,* Nicky thought. *He's a good yeller.* Instead of feeling hot, she just felt warm. She smiled. *He can yell every bit as well as Mr. Ring.*

When the fifteen minutes were up Nicky shyly walked back to the livingroom. Only Lisa was there.

"Where is he?" Nicky asked.

Lisa started to laugh. "Do you know what was eating him?" she asked.

"My shoes?" Nicky said.

"No. This is the first Sunday *ever* that he hasn't been to church. He was having all these guilt feelings. So I sent him down in time for the last mass."

"Is that what was wrong? Gee. You could have gone with him. I wouldn't have minded," Nicky said.

"Maybe next time," Lisa said. "He needed to go alone today."

"I liked him — even when he yelled at me," Nicky said. "Not at first maybe. But when I thought about it."

"Oh, you nut," Lisa said.

When Alex came back from church, he and Nicky were shy with each other for awhile. But soon things were back to normal, and they ate a long lunch on the patio, and Alex talked again about how he was really going to bring them down to southern California soon. And sometime during the lunch, Nicky didn't know exactly when, she found herself calling Alex, *Dads*, and he and her mother didn't even let on that they noticed.

Alex stayed till six before he walked down the hill to begin his hitch to the Valley.

As Nicky watched him go, she thought, *Dads will fix things. I know we'll all be together real soon.*

* 15 *

Several weeks later, Mrs. Ketcher was sitting at her desk in the front of the classroom. There was a thick pile of papers on the desk. Mrs. Ketcher's right hand rested on the pile of papers, and her left hand dipped the small brush into the open red nail polish bottle and touched up her nicked nails.

"These papers all have to go home," Mrs. Ketcher said. "And they have to come back *signed by a parent.* I have never in all my years of teaching seen such poor results on a math test. 80% of you got E. *E,*" Mrs. Ketcher repeated. "19% got D. *D!* 1% got C–. *Minus!* And I want you to bring them back tomorrow, signed, and I want to know what your parents said about it."

Nicky's throat felt odd, as if there were two golf balls lodged in it. She squirmed down in her seat. Her left eye began to twitch. She put her hand up to cover it. *E!* That was failure. That was unbelievable. That was unforgivable.

Going home on the school bus with their math papers clasped in their hands, Nicky and Gay didn't have much to say.

Finally Nicky saw a tear moving past Gay's nose.

"Well, you only got D," she said to Gay. "How do you think I feel?"

"But I'm good at math," Gay said.

"Well I am, too."

"I know you are. But I'm really good. It's my best subject. You're good at lots of things. But I'm only good at math. I'm going to teach math when I grow up or work in a bank or something like that."

"Oh, that dumb old Mrs. Ketcher," Nicky said.

"Now I'm not good at anything," Gay said.

"Oh, Gay," Nicky said. But she was so depressed herself she couldn't think of anything to cheer up Gay.

Nicky decided she'd show her mother the math paper right away, anything to get it over with. But when she got home, she found Lisa completely distraught. Her friend Gladys was there, and they were both exclaiming about the headlines in the local papers.

**THE HIDDEN WOMAN
IN FATHER POLITAN'S LIFE
PRIEST IS SECRETLY MARRIED!
LOVE MORE IMPORTANT THAN MIGRANTS**

There were pictures, too, of all of them.

"When did they take this one?" Nicky asked, pointing to a rather blurred one of her and Lisa.

"From the background it looks like you were coming out of the grocery market," Gladys said.

"Listen, Glad," Lisa said, "you've been a dream today. I couldn't have made it without you. But Nicky's home now. She can get the phone calls. Those darn reporters. I want to talk to Alex!"

"Now take it easy," Gladys said. "Look, I'll go home now, but have Nicky run over if you need me. O.K.? Sure?"

Lisa nodded. "Thanks a million, Glad."

When Gladys left, Nicky asked, "What's going to happen now?"

Lisa slumped into the chaise. "The whole world is tumbling down on us. The dam broke."

"How did they find out about Dads being married to you?"

"Somebody must have seen him with us and started asking questions. Who knows? I think today he just lost everything he ever gained for the migrant workers. And you know what's funny? What really takes the cake? One article says even *they* don't like him anymore. Because of us. Because he married."

"Gee, Mom," Nicky said.

"If I could just talk to Alex. If he could get to a phone. He needs me. I know it. I'm helpless."

The phone rang.

"If it isn't Alex, hang up," Lisa said. "And don't answer the front door. There was one reporter out there knocking for two hours today."

Nicky picked up the phone. It wasn't Alex. She hung up.

"He's such a good guy," Lisa said. "He didn't need all this publicity. He was going to tell them, quietly, when he was ready."

"Oh, Mom," Nicky said. She put her hand on Lisa's shoulder. Lisa grabbed it and cried into it.

All evening Lisa paced back and forth, crying, worrying, wringing her hands. Gladys brought them spaghetti. If she hadn't, they would probably have forgotten to eat. As it was, they couldn't eat much anyhow. It just wouldn't go down.

There was no word from Alex. Lisa was hysterical, and Nicky felt ill, about Alex and about the fact she hadn't found the moment to tell her mother about the E and to get her to sign the math paper.

They tried to watch TV. But Lisa couldn't stand it. She clicked it off.

At midnight, Lisa insisted that Nicky go to bed.

"At least, try to sleep, baby," she said.

"What about you, Mom?"

"I'll never sleep. Never. I'll make a pot of coffee. Maybe Alex will hitch a ride up here. Maybe he'll call. I need him so badly."

"Let me stay up with you," Nicky begged.

"Baby, you've got school tomorrow."

"Well. . ." Nicky said.

"Nicky, what is it? You've got something on your mind," Lisa said.

Nicky thrust the math test at Lisa. Her hands were shaking so badly, Lisa had to hold the papers herself to see what they were.

"You have to sign it, and I have to take it back tomorrow and tell Mrs. Ketcher what you said."

"An E? Is this an E? On a math test?" Lisa asked.

Nicky nodded.

Lisa threw her arms around Nicky and hugged her. "Oh baby, that's fabulous!" she shouted.

"What?" Nicky said.

But Lisa couldn't explain because she had started to laugh. She laughed loud and hard, and she seemed like she wouldn't stop laughing. She held her stomach and doubled up on the sofa and laughed and giggled and laughed.

"Mother, are you hysterical?" Nicky whispered.

That set Lisa off again.

"Yes!" she shouted. "Yes, I'm hysterically happy."

"What should I tell Mrs. Ketcher?" Nicky asked.

Lisa's eyes fell on the newspaper headlines, and suddenly she became sober. She swished the newspapers onto the floor and stomped on them. Then she found a pen and wrote Lisa Politan in a big flourish on the math test. She solemnly looked at Nicky.

"You found out today you aren't perfect. I'm so glad. When Mrs. Ketcher asks what I said about the math paper, just tell her I laughed. That's all."

"I should say you laughed?" Nicky said, incredulously.

"Yes. And now I really want you to go to bed."

Nicky started to shake. "Do you think Dads will call?"

"I hope so, baby," Lisa said. "Hey, you're shaking. Are you O.K.? Why are you so upset? You weren't half as upset over the art contest."

"But then I knew I was the best."

"And now?"

"I have an awful hard time getting good grades in math. Art comes easy to me. But math — I have to work and work and work at it."

"Don't fight it, Nicky. I don't know what you're trying to prove. Honestly, I don't. You don't have to be perfect in math to prove anything to me. You don't have to prove anything to Alex. I don't understand what drives you. Who do you have to prove something to?"

Nicky picked at the third fingernail on her left hand. She twisted the hair by her ear. She looked at the beige rug.

"When Daddy left," she said softly, "I thought it was something I did. I decided I'd be perfect. I'd do everything right and everything the best, and there would be nothing I couldn't do. Everyone would like me, and no one would ever leave a great person like me, again."

"Oh God, Nicky. Oh my sweet baby," Lisa said. "You are great. You're the greatest person in the world."

Lisa hugged Nicky and walked her to the bedroom. She kissed her left eyebrow. "Sleep, my sweet baby. Forget. Forget. I love you. Alex loves you. Sleep, my sweet baby. Rennie's flown away with the wind. He doesn't matter anymore. Sleep. In the morning everything will be all right."

* 16 *

Nicky was awakened by the alarm clock. She turned it off as she swung out of bed and into her pink slippers.

"Mom!" she called. "Mom!"

She walked through the house. From the living room window she saw Lisa painting in the back yard. The morning paper was on the coffee table. Nicky picked it up and read the headline:

PRIEST TO SEEK ANNULMENT

She ran to the patio door, opened it and leaned out.

"Mom!" she called.

Lisa waved. Nicky walked out to her. The dew on the grass stained her slippers, but she was glad to have them on when she felt the crunch of snails beneath them as she walked across to Lisa.

"Mom, what's an annulment?" she said to Lisa.

Lisa turned. Somehow she didn't look pretty. Dark gray masses were beneath her pink swollen eyes.

"You haven't slept!" Nicky said. "Did Dads come? What's an annulment?"

Lisa turned back to her painting. "An annulment is a paper that says two people aren't married."

"You mean like a divorce?"

"Sort of," Lisa said.

"Oh, Mom. Not again. We don't want to be divorced again. So soon. Oh, Mom. Say no. Don't let it happen."

"Do you see how these two colors mix, Nicky?" Lisa said. "This is one of the best days we've had. No pollution. I bet we can see twenty miles. Look at San Pablo Bay. Look at Hamilton Air Force Base. Terra Linda. Look over there. See how far we can see today. Isn't it beautiful? Don't we have the most beautiful view in the world? I'm going to paint it all today, every little bay tree."

"Dads didn't call?"

"No."

"Maybe the paper is just making it up."

"I doubt it. He could have, should have, called by now. In a way it's for the best. I couldn't stand in the way of all those migrant farm workers. He's done so much for them. Why should that go down the drain? We had a few good months. I wouldn't want whole families to go back to living in their cars. That's what Alex took them out of into modest but decent homes; he arranged for medical care, schooling and day care for the children, better working conditions for the parents. Why should one person's happiness send them back to living in their cars? They need Alex more than I do."

Nicky went back and phoned Gladys to come and stay with Lisa for the day. Then she ate breakfast and went to school with her signed math test.

"Harold will collect the signed math tests," Mrs. Ketcher said, examining a small run in her nylons. "I trust you all got them signed?"

She took the papers from Harold. "Thank you, Harold. Now, we'll begin here," she said, pointing to the first row. "Stand up and speak clearly. All right, Alison. You begin. What did your parents say about your D?"

Bony Alison stood up. She looked at Mrs. Ketcher's red shoes. "I'm not allowed to watch TV for a week," she said. Then she sat down.

"Tony?" Mrs. Ketcher said.

Tony had to do the dishes three nights in a row.

"Gay?"

Gay had to do math problems for an hour every day after school. Finally, Mrs. Ketcher got to the third row where Nicky sat.

"Nicky?" she said, smoothing out the wrinkles in her red dress.

Nicky stood up. Her neck felt like it was painted Alizarin Crimson.

"My mom," Nicky said, "just laughed."

Nicky could hear Ernestine giggle.

"She what?" Mrs. Ketcher said.

"She laughed," Nicky said.

"Well!" Mrs. Ketcher said, yanking down her girdle. "Well!" she said, putting her hands on her hips and sucking in her breath.

Her chest rose with the effort and her stomach disappeared until Nicky realized Mrs. Ketcher, with her white hair and her red dress, had assumed the shape of the Heinz ketchup bottle — ketchup lover's size.

"Well!" Mrs. Ketcher said. Yank. Yank. "Well!" She yanked again. "I think we've spent enough time on this. Let's get on to science. Get out your books. *And don't anyone make a sound.*"

Several of the kids were smiling but Nicky felt bad about Mrs. Ketcher. *She's really a very nice person,* Nicky thought, *but she takes things too seriously.*

Nicky didn't get too much teasing at school that day, but a few boys came around at recess and asked, "How's it feel to have a priest for a father?" and "How's it feel to have a Father for a father?" She was glad to get home to Lisa.

And there was news. Somehow Alex had gotten a note to Lisa through a friend of a friend of a friend. All the note said was that Alex would try to get to her, probably sometime after midnight.

"Oh, let me stay up!" Nicky begged.

"Listen, honey. This is no fun visit. Alex is decent. He's going to tell me in person about this annulment business. This is serious stuff."

"But he's my father! I want to see him!" Nicky said.

"I can't promise," Lisa said.

* 17 *

Nicky went to her room. She picked up her pink bathrobe and hung it up. She carefully lined her shoes in the closet. She cleaned out her underwear and sock drawer. She dusted the furniture and vacuumed the floor.

Everybody leaves me, she thought. *Everybody leaves my mother. She has such rotten luck with men.*

Nicky went into her mother's bedroom and made the bed.

"She never makes the bed," Nicky said. "She never picks up her clothes. They all land on chairs."

Nicky hung up some of Lisa's clothes and put the others in a pile by the door. Then when she had dusted and vacuumed Lisa's room, she took the dirty clothes to the garage and started a load of wash in the machine.

"Look at the piles," she said. "There are piles and piles of dirty clothes. There's almost no room for the car."

She went to the living room and started dusting.

My mother doesn't know how to keep a man. If there's one thing I'm going to learn, it's how to keep one. Why do they keep leaving?

She vacuumed the rug.

It isn't that I'm not a great person. I've been a perfect daughter. But still they go away.

She scrubbed the bathroom and tidied up the dining room. When she got to the kitchen, Lisa had the paints spread out over everything. They were on the table, the counter space, the stove.

How can you be so messy? Nicky thought.

Lisa looked up and smiled. "Hi kid. I hear the washing machine running. Nesting instinct?"

"I don't know," Nicky said. "What is it?"

"It's what I get about once a month when you see me running around like a madwoman scrubbing every little corner."

"I don't remember seeing you do that," Nicky said.

"My, aren't we testy," Lisa said. "Would you like to speak to the complaint bureau?"

"Well, you say you think Dads will be here. But you just leave everything looking a mess. Why don't you clean up? Why do I have to do it?"

"Hey, you don't have to do it. Did I ask you to do anything?" Lisa said.

"Well, somebody's got to do it," Nicky said.

"Why?"

Nicky was exasperated. She threw up her arms. "Because!" she said.

"Look, Nicky, we better get something straight. I don't have to impress Alex. How the house looks isn't going to affect the annulment one way or the other. He knows me. He's going to be awfully surprised to see a clean house. And frankly, I wish you hadn't bothered."

"But I thought it should look nice," Nicky said.

"Nicky, I've been given a talent. And you've been given it, too. We're artists, and we must practice and encourage our talents every moment we can. Some people like to clean house. Some people can *only* clean house. But we can't let their ideas of how a house should look be forced on us. Our talent is more important than that. Don't do what other people think you should do. Don't follow their standards. That road leads to ulcers and indigestion. Follow your natural tendencies. And whatever happens, well, it happens. But above all else, you've got to be free to be yourself."

"I guess you don't want me to clean the kitchen?" Nicky said.

"Oh, you scamp! No, I don't," Lisa said, smiling.

"Your picture's nice," Nicky said.

"So are you," Lisa said.

Nicky hesitated in the doorway. "If I started the wash, maybe I should finish it?" she whispered.

"If you don't let me work, I'm going to throw this whole tube of Sky Blue at you. Do the wash if you want. Don't do it if you don't want. You are free to choose!"

Nicky wandered out to the garage. She took Lisa's clothes out of the washer and put them in the dryer.

I've been so perfect, she thought. She put another pile of dirty clothes in the washing machine. *And what good has it done? I don't think anybody's noticed but me.*

She put the soap in the machine and turned it on.

"Will the real Nicky Politan please stand up?" she said.

She tilted her head and thought a moment. *Hey girl,* she said to herself, *what would you do if you thought Dads might be here tonight?*

In a moment, she knew. She ran to the kitchen and made a place for herself beside Lisa.

She got out her paints and set up her easel. She chose a small size canvas board and began to paint an orange.

It won't be a perfect circle, that's for sure. This will be a real orange, lopsided and lumpy and delicious.

In two hours she was finished and satisfied. The orange certainly wasn't a perfect circle. It had indentations and a bump at one end. It wasn't perfect at all. It was just an orange.

Nicky wrote a note and tacked it on the easel next to the painting.

Dear Dads,

This is for you. Nobody's perfect, not even this orange. But I ate the model after I painted it, and it was good and juicy, and I loved it, even though it wasn't perfect. I want to see you. Please wake me up.

Love,

Nicky

P.S. If you get the urge to clutch this picture to your bosom, DON'T. The paint's still wet.

* 18 *

"Nicole," the voice said, softly. "Nicole!"

She felt large fingers on her forehead and again heard the "Nicole!"

She sat up and threw her arms around the big man sitting at the foot of her bed. His brown wooly sweater tickled her nose, but she didn't care. Only one person called her Nicole. Alex.

"Dads," Nicky said. "Oh, Dads. Thanks for waking me up."

"That's a beautiful painting you made for me, Nicole," Alex said.

"It was just an orange."

"It's a fantastic orange. Now, what did *you* want to see *me* about?"

"I just wanted to tell you I love you. I'll always love you, even if you annul us."

Alex put his fist to her chin. "Funny, you two girls are quite a bit alike. That's just what your mother says. Lisa's making coffee. You're not too sleepy, are you? Want to have a glass of milk and listen to our talk?"

"Do I!" Nicky said. She rushed to the closet, grabbed her pink robe and threw it over her pajamas. She took Alex's hand.

"I'll walk you to the kitchen," she said.

Lisa was moving her paints so they could sit at the kitchen table.

"You look tired. You've been through a lot these two days," Alex said to her.

"And you, Alex, what has it been like for you?" Lisa said.

"What I expected, really; everything except those awful headlines. But it's my fault. I should have told them before the newspapers dug the story out and spread it over the front pages. I should have quietly resigned months ago."

"What did they say?" Lisa asked.

"I've been a priest for twenty-one years. Now I'm an ex-priest. It took a long time to say it, but that's what it boils down to," Alex said.

"So what happens?" Lisa said. "I'm going crazy wondering. Here have some more coffee. Nicky, want a cookie?"

"So what happens is this," Alex said. "I have several choices."

"Annulment," Lisa said.

"That was a nasty headline. Are you crazy? Do you think I'd annul this beautiful marriage? Look, there's no sense in going through my whole two days. First of all I apologize for not coming to you sooner. Please understand I couldn't. Second, let me tell you what I've decided to do."

"Alex, before you say anything else, I want it perfectly understood that your work with the migrants comes before me and Nicky, and I will understand if you decide for them," Lisa said.

Alex smiled. "You say that beautifully with tears rolling down your cheeks," he teased. "You two are an absolute mess! Don't you know I love you? Annulment never entered my head. Some headline writer thought that up! I'm an ex-priest now. *EX*. I can do anything I want. I can sell insurance. I can become a short-order cook. I can run for mayor of Los Angeles! But mostly, I want to keep doing what I was doing, with your help. What would you say if I tell you I think I can do more for the migrants now than before? And I don't mean just me. I mean all of us. My family. You, Lisa. You, Nicole. My team!"

"What can I do, Dads?" Nicky said.

"Well, you and Lisa will come down to the San Joaquin Valley to live with me, won't you? I have great plans, fantastic plans, and the bishop is going to help me with them. I'm not part of the church, but the church is still part of me. I'm going to be a lay person, working for the church in almost the same ways I did as a priest. I won't have any religious duties, but I'll be teaching and organizing and so busy with all my plans! We're going to set up a new day-care center for the children, tutoring centers for school-age children, and field hospitals and medical facilities. Lisa can teach painting! What do you say?"

"Oh, Alex," Lisa said. "When can we start?"

"Nicole?" Alex asked.

"Boy, I can't wait," Nicky said.

"Then I want you to jump into bed and go back to sleep. Lisa and I will work out the details. We'll tell you about it in the morning."

Nicky threw her arms around Alex. "Goodnight, Dads. Goodnight, Mom," she said.

As she headed back to her bedroom, she could hear Alex say, "I could make a lot more money selling insurance. Are you sure you won't mind, Lisa? This house will be a castle compared to what we'll be living in."

"I don't care. I don't care. I don't care," her mother said.

"Some of my people, well, it's hard for them to accept a priest's leaving the priesthood. I've heard remarks about 'the hussy' who drove me out of the priesthood," Alex said.

"I'll become friends with them," Lisa said. "I'll prove I'm just a woman like other wives. I'll explain that love is something that happens no matter how hard you try to stop it. If that doesn't work, I'll punch them in the nose," she said.

Nicky could hear Lisa and Alex giggling. She kicked off her slippers and fell asleep with a smile.

* 19 *

The next day Nicky went through her closet looking for all her animal toys and dolls. As she
brought them out, she shook them off and placed
them on the bed next to Old Teddy Bear.

There was Felix the giraffe, the boa constrictor from the carnival that she had named Clutch,
Emil the camel, Gertrude the bride doll, Pirouette
the French doll, the Barbie doll and her friends,
the two plastic monkeys named Monk and
Monk-Monk, and six horse statues.

She crossed her legs and sat on the bed with
them.

"Hey, you want to know something?" she
asked them. "We're moving."

She put her elbow on her knee and held up
her chin with her hand.

"Do you want to ask me something? Go
ahead. Ask."

Three horse statues fell over. Nicky set them up again. Then she took Clutch and wound him all around the toys.

"Now if you fall you won't get hurt," she told the horses.

She stared at the toys.

"Look, if nobody is going to ask any questions, you won't know anything. Aren't you curious? Aren't you?"

Two horse statues fell over.

"Honestly," Nicky said. "I should just let you lie there, but . . ."

She set them up again.

"Now attention. Everyone listen. Old Teddy Bear wants to know what our new house will be like. Well, we don't know yet. We'll live at a motel for a few weeks until we find a house. But when we do, I don't think it will be as nice as this one, but we don't care about that, do we? And the motel will be fun. We'll have a little kitchen there so we can make our own meals. Don't ask where my mother will put her paints. Just don't ask."

Nicky leaned over and picked up Pirouette.

"Dear Pirou," she said, "I can see you have a question. You want to know when the moving company will get here. My dear, you have been watching too much TV. There won't be a moving company. We're going to do it ourselves. We have to pack everything in boxes, and Dads will rent a big truck. We'll put the furniture and boxes on the truck. We'll drive it down south into a big warehouse where they store things. We'll leave everything there while we live at the motel, and then we'll pick it up when we get our new house."

Nicky put Pirouette back with the group and picked up Barbie and all her friends.

"I know your question. Will we have any friends? Probably not for awhile. We might have lonely days when we wish we could be back here playing with Gay or even wish we could be going to school at Sun View again. It's not easy to make friends living in a motel. But when we get our new house, we'll find new friends. Where Dads works, there will be lots of children. Some might like us, and some might not. Some might be shy, but we'll be friendly, won't we? We might even learn to speak Spanish. Dads can speak Spanish, and we want to learn too, don't we? Adios. Buenos noches. See, I'm learning already. Buenos dias."

Nicky laid Barbie and her friends back with their heads resting on Clutch.

"Hey, Emil," she said to the camel, "you'll like the weather. Hey, Felix, the answer to your question — will this still be our house? — no, we're going to sell it. That's a funny feeling isn't it, Felix?"

Nicky jumped off the bed and ran to the garage. She took one of the many boxes there that Alex and Lisa had begged from the grocery store. Her box said Campbell's Cheddar Cheese Soup on the side. She grabbed some newspapers from the kitchen.

Back in the bedroom, she started putting her toys in the box. She wrapped the breakable toys in newspapers. There was some space left at the top of the box. She opened her first dresser drawer and put its contents in the box — her jewelry, a deck of cards, three yellow pencils, two books — *Mandy* and *Ong, The Wild Gander* — and last year's school picture.

The Campbell's Cheddar Cheese Soup box was filled. She closed the lid. It opened. She went back to the kitchen for tape and string and the black magic marker. She tied and taped the box and marked it TOYS ETC. — NICKY'S ROOM.

She bent toward the bottom of the box and called into it, "Hey, Old Teddy Bear. I can hear you asking if we're going to be happy there."

She looked up at the ceiling of her room. "I sure hope so. I sure do hope so," she said, quietly.

Then Nicky ran out on the patio and called to Lisa and Alex.

"I packed my first box! I'm ready to go!"

* 20 *

They would be moving to the San Joaquin Valley
on the weekend. Nicky felt there were a few
things she should clear up before they left. The
first was with Mrs. Ketcher. So one day she waited
after school till all the kids were out of the classroom.

"Mrs. Ketcher, I want to apologize for my bad
mark on that math test. I didn't mean to embarrass
you by what I said. I mean, my mother did laugh.
But if you knew what we were going through at
the time! Anyhow, I hope you understand. You're
really one of my favorite teachers."

"I do understand, Nicky," Mrs. Ketcher said.
"And I wish you all the best of luck. I've gotten to
thinking about it. You know, if everyone scored
low, either the test was no good or I didn't teach it
well enough. I've decided to forget those grades. I

think you'll come out very well in your final mark."

And then, Nicky wanted to have a talk with Gay. She was able to say what she wanted to say one morning on the school bus.

"I'm going to miss you, Gay. I don't guess I'll ever have as good a friend as you."

"You write me first because I don't know your address," Gay said.

"O.K. And you know, Gay, I hope someday you'll write that you got brave and pinned your hair back for the whole world to see your birthmark."

"Well, I won't," Gay said.

"Well, you might someday, mightn't you?" Nicky said.

"Don't hold your breath waiting for it to happen," Gay said.

And then, there was Ernestine. She had not begged Nicky for anything since the zoo affair. Even though Ernestine had been a mess all through school, Nicky had known her a long time and felt she should say something to her — at least, goodbye. But somehow she never got around to it. In fact, she forgot about it.

When Alex arrived with the big truck to move all their things, Nicky was busy hauling boxes and her bicycle and scooter to load into it.

Suddenly, somebody, hot and dirty and dusty, was standing by the truck as Nicky jumped off. Ernestine.

"Hi!" Ernestine said.

"Oh, hi," Nicky said. "We're leaving today."

"I can see," Ernestine said. "Can you take everything? D'you have to leave any old toys behind?"

"We'll have room for everything," Nicky said.

"My mother's sick," Ernestine said.

"I have all this packing to do," Nicky said. "I'll have to say goodbye. If you're ever in the Valley, come by and see us." She started walking to the house.

Ernestine followed her. "Boy, is she sick. We called the doctor but he won't come. I don't know what we can do. If I only had something to cheer her up. Your mother have any perfume? Just a little bottle or half a bottle? She's so sick she wouldn't know the difference."

Nicky stepped in the front door. She thought about her mother's dresser. It was always full of perfume bottles. She thought of Mrs. Ring, sick. She thought how nice it would be on her last day to do one more nice thing for Ernestine. Ernestine would probably always remember her as a wonderful, wonderful person.

"Are you going to give me some perfume?" Ernestine said.

"Ernestine," Nicky said. "BUG OFF!" She slammed the door and went to get another box to load on the truck.

Phyllis Green, the author of seven other books for young people, was formerly a special education teacher. Her experiences — some poignant, some frustrating, many inspiring — gave birth to *Walkie-Talkie*, another book for Addison-Wesley.

Ice River, also for Addison-Wesley, was awarded a First Prize for Picture Books by the Council of Wisconsin Writers. *Wild Violets* was a Junior Literary Guild Selection. *Mildred Murphy, How Does Your Garden Grow?* has received warm praise for its engaging treatment of friendship, the problems of the elderly and the importance of caring.